To Anna
With love from Howard
Christmas 1994.

THE
BEDTIME
BOOK

For Kate and Alice – P.I.

First published in Great Britain in 1992 by
Frances Lincoln Limited, Apollo Works
5 Charlton Kings Road, London NW5 2SB

British Library Cataloguing in Publication Data
available on request

ISBN 0-7112-0681-3

Printed and bound in Italy

1 3 5 7 9 8 6 4 2

THE BEDTIME BOOK

Stories and poems to read aloud

CHOSEN BY **Kathy Henderson**

ILLUSTRATED BY **Penny Ives**

FRANCES LINCOLN

CONTENTS
(including story-telling times)

Dream Variations

LANGSTON HUGHES

To fling my arms wide
In some place of the sun,
To whirl and to dance
Till the white day is done.
Then rest at cool evening
Beneath a tall tree
While Night comes on gently,
    Dark like me –
That is my dream!

To fling my arms wide
In the face of the sun,
Dance! Whirl! Whirl!
Till the quick day is done.
Rest at pale evening . . .
A tall, slim tree . . .
Night coming tenderly
    Black like me.

Girls and Boys Come Out to Play

TRADITIONAL RHYME

Girls and boys,
Come out to play,
The moon doth shine,
As bright as day.
Leave your supper
And leave your sleep
And join your playfellows
In the street.
Come with a whoop,
Come with a call,
Come with a good will,
Or not at all.
Up the ladder
And down the wall,
A ha'penny loaf
Will serve us all.
You find milk
And I'll find flour,
And we'll have a pudding
In half an hour.

The Crow and the Daylight

TRADITIONAL INUIT STORY retold by Norah Montgomerie

LONG, long ago, when the world was young, there was no daylight in Alaska. It was dark all the time. The people of Alaska lived in the dark, managing as well as they could. They had only their seal-oil lamps for light.

In one village lived a crow. The people liked this crow, and thought he was very wise. He told them wonderful stories of the things he had seen and done on his long journeys in distant lands.

One day he seemed very sad and did not speak at all. The people wondered what was troubling him.

"Crow, what makes you so sad?" they asked.

"I'm sad for all you people in Alaska," said the crow, "because you have no daylight."

"What is daylight?" they asked. "What is it like? We've never even heard of it."

"Well," said the crow, "if you had daylight in Alaska, you could go anywhere and see everything."

This seemed very wonderful to them.

"Please fetch us some daylight, dear crow," they begged.

"I'm afraid that is impossible," said the crow.

"Why is that?" asked the people.

"Well, I know where it is," said the crow, "but it would be far too difficult to bring it here."

13

The people all crowded round and begged him to bring them some daylight.

"Oh, crow, you are so clever," said their chief, "we know you can do this for us."

"Very well, I will go," said the crow at last, "and see what I can do."

Next day he spread his wings and flew towards the east. He flew on and on, in the dark, till his wings ached, but he never stopped.

After he had flown for many days, the sky gradually grew lighter, until at last daylight filled the whole sky.

Perching on a tree, he looked about him to find where the light came from. At last he saw it shining from a big snow-house in a village.

Now in the snow-house lived the chief of the village, and he had a beautiful daughter. She came out of the house every day to fetch water from the ice-hole in the river, the only place Eskimos can find fresh water in winter.

The crow slipped off his skin and hid it by the entrance of the house. Then he covered himself with magic dust, and said some magic words which sounded like this:

Ya-ka-ty, ta-ka-ty, na-ka-ty!
A tiny speck of dust I'll be,
Then nobody will notice me!

He sat on a sunbeam in a crack near the door, and waited for the chief's daughter. When she came back from the river, the crow, who looked just like a speck of dust, lighted on her dress and passed with her into the house where the daylight was. There was a small boy playing on the floor, surrounded by little toys of walrus ivory. They were tiny dogs, foxes, kayaks and little walrus heads. He kept putting the toys into the box and spilling them out again.

The chief watched his little son proudly, but did not notice the speck of dust that drifted down to the little boy's ear. (The dust was the crow, of course. Remember?)

Soon the child began to cry.

"What do you want, little son?" asked the chief.

"Ask for the daylight to play with," whispered the crow into the little boy's ear. So the child asked for the daylight.

"Give him what he asks for," said the chief to his daughter.

She fetched a hunting bag, and took from it a small wooden box, out of which she took a bright shining ball, and gave it to the child.

He liked the ball and played with it for a long time. But the crow wanted to get hold of it, so he whispered in the child's ear, "Ask for string to tie on it."

"I want string on my ball," demanded the little boy.

At once a piece of string was tied to the ball.

When the chief and his daughter went out, the crow whispered in the little boy's ear, "Take your ball to the entrance."

So the little boy took his ball of daylight to the very place at the entrance where the crow had left his skin.

The speck of dust slipped back into the crow's skin, and became a real crow again. Seizing the string in his beak the crow flew away, leaving the child howling.

The cries brought the chief and his daughter and all the people of the village running to see what was wrong, and there, high in the sky, they saw the crow flying away with their precious daylight. They tried to shoot him down with their arrows, but he was too far away, and was soon out of sight.

When the crow reached the land of Alaska, he thought he would try the daylight to see how it worked. Passing over the first dark village, he scratched a little bit off the daylight. It fell on the village and gave it bright light.

16

At every village he came to he did the same, until he reached his very own village. Hovering over it, he broke the daylight into little bits, scattering them far and wide.

The people greeted him with shouts. They were so happy they danced and sang, and prepared a great feast in his honour. They were so grateful to him they couldn't thank him enough for bringing his gift of daylight.

To this very day the people of Alaska are grateful to the crow, and never try to shoot him.

I'm the Big Sleeper

MICHAEL ROSEN

I'm the big sleeper
rolled up in his sheets
at the break of day

I'm a big sleeper living soft
in a hard kind of way

the light through the curtain
can't wake me
I'm under the blankets
you can't shake me
the pillow rustler
and blanket gambler
a mean tough eiderdown man

I keep my head
I stay in bed

I Like to Stay Up

GRACE NICHOLS

I like to stay up
and listen
when big people talking
jumbie stories

Ooooooooooooooooooh
I does feel so tingly
and excited
inside – eeeeeeeeeee

But when my mother say
"Girl, time for bed"
then is when
I does feel a dread
then is when
I does jump into me bed
then is when
I does cover up
from me feet to me head

then is when
I does wish
I didn't listen
to no stupid jumbie story
then is when
I does wish
I did read me book instead

jumbie: ghost

The Fly-by-night

TERRY JONES

A LITTLE girl was lying in bed one night when she heard a tapping on her window. She was rather frightened, but she went to the window and opened it, telling herself that it was probably just the wind. But when she looked out, do you know what she saw? It was a little creature as black as soot, with bright yellow eyes, and it was sitting on a cat that appeared to be flying.

"Hello," said the creature, "would you like to come flying?"

"Yes, *please!*" said the little girl, and she climbed out of the window on to the cat and off they flew.

"Hang on tight!" cried the creature.

"Where are we going?" asked the little girl.

"I don't know!" called the creature.

"Who are you?" asked the little girl.

"I haven't got a name," said the creature, "I'm just a fly-by-night!"

And up they went into the air, over the hills and away.

The little girl looked around her at the bright moon, and the stars that seemed to wink at her and chuckle to themselves. Then she looked down at the black world below her, and she was suddenly frightened again, and said, "How will we find our way back?"

"Oh! Don't worry about *that*!" cried the fly-by-night. "What does it matter?" And he leaned on the cat's whiskers and down they swooped towards the dark earth.

"But I must be able to get home!" cried the little girl. "My mother and father will wonder where I am!"

"Oh! Poop-de-doo!" cried the fly-by-night, and he pulled back on the cat's whiskers and up they soared – up and up into the stars again, and all the stars were humming in rhythm:

> Boodle-dum-dee
> Boodle-dum-da,
> Isn't it great,
> Being a star!

And all the stars had hands, and they started clapping together in unison.

Then suddenly the moon opened his mouth and sang in a loud booming voice:

> I'm just the moon,
> But that's fine by me
> As long as I hear that
> Boodle-dum-dee!

And the cat opened its mouth wide and sang, "Wheeeeeeee!" and they looped-the-loop and turned circles to the rhythm of the stars.

But the little girl started to cry and said, "Oh please, I want to go home!"

"Oh no, you don't!" cried the fly-by-night, and took the cat straight up as fast as they could go, and the stars seemed to flash past them like silver darts.

"Please!" cried the little girl. "Take me back!"

"Spoilsport!" yelled the fly-by-night and he stopped the cat dead, then tipped it over, and down they swooped so fast that they left their stomachs behind them at the top, and landed on a silent hill.

"Here you are!" said the fly-by-night.

"But this isn't my home," said the little girl, looking around at the dark, lonely countryside.

"Oh! It'll be around somewhere, I expect," said the fly-by-night.

"But we've come miles and miles from my home!" cried the little girl. But it was too late. The fly-by-night had pulled back on the cat's whiskers and away he soared up into the night sky, and the last the little girl saw of him was a black shape silhouetted against the moon.

The little girl shivered and looked around her, wondering if there were any wild animals about.

"Which way should I go?" she wondered.

"Try the path through the wood," said a stone at her feet. So she set off along the path that led through the dark wood.

As soon as she got amongst the trees, the leaves blotted out the light of the moon, branches clutched at her hair, and roots tried to trip up her feet, and she thought she heard the trees snigger, quietly; and they seemed to say to each other, "That'll teach her to go off with a fly-by-night!"

Suddenly she felt a cold hand gripping her neck, but it was just a cobweb strung with dew. And she heard the spider busy itself with repairs, muttering, "Tut-tut-tut-tut. She went off with a fly-by-night! Tut-tut-tut-tut."

As the little girl peered into the wood, she thought she could see eyes watching her and winking to each other, and little voices you couldn't really hear whispered under the broad leaves,

"What a silly girl – to go off with a fly-by-night! She should have known better! Tut-tut-tut-tut."

Eventually she felt so miserable and so foolish that she just sat down and cried by a still pond.

"Now then, what's the matter?" said a kindly voice.

The little girl looked up, and then all around her, but she couldn't see anyone. "Who's that?" she asked.

"Look in the pond," said the voice, and she looked down and saw the reflection of the moon, smiling up at her out of the pond.

"Don't take on so," said the moon.

"But I've been so silly," said the little girl, "and now I'm quite, quite lost and I don't know how I'll *ever* get home."

"You'll get home all right," said the moon's reflection. "Hop on a lily-pad and follow me."

So the little girl stepped cautiously on to a lily-pad, and the moon's reflection started to move slowly across the pond, and down a stream, and the little girl paddled the lily-pad after it.

Slowly and silently they slipped through the night forest, and then out into the open fields they followed the stream, until they came to a hill she recognized, and suddenly there was her own house. She ran as fast as she could and climbed in through the window of her own room, and snuggled into her own dear bed.

And the moon smiled in at her through the window, and she fell asleep thinking how silly she'd been to go off with the fly-by-night. But, you know, somewhere, deep down inside her, she half hoped she'd hear another tap on her window one day, and find another fly-by-night offering her a ride on its flying cat.

But she never did.

Bump

SPIKE MILLIGAN

Things that go "bump" in the night,
Should not really give one a fright.
It's the hole in each ear
That lets in the fear,
That, and the absence of light!

The Adventures of Isabel

OGDEN NASH

Isabel met an enormous bear,
Isabel, Isabel, didn't care;
The bear was hungry, the bear was ravenous,
The bear's big mouth was cruel and cavernous.
The bear said, "Isabel, glad to meet you,
How do, Isabel, now I'll eat you!"
Isabel, Isabel, didn't worry,
Isabel didn't scream or scurry,
She washed her hands and she straightened her hair up,
Then Isabel quietly ate the bear up.

Once on a night as black as pitch
Isabel met a wicked witch.
The witch's face was cross and wrinkled,
The witch's gums with teeth were sprinkled.
"Ho Ho, Isabel!" the old witch crowed,
"I'll turn you into an ugly toad!"
Isabel, Isabel, didn't worry,
Isabel didn't scream or scurry,
She showed no rage, she showed no rancour,
But she turned the witch into milk and drank her.

Isabel once was asleep in bed
When a horrible dream crawled into her head.
It was worse than a dinosaur, worse than a shark,
Worse than an octopus oozing in the dark.
"Boo!" said the dream, with a dreadful grin,
"I'm going to scare you out of your skin!"
Isabel, Isabel, didn't worry,
Isabel didn't scream or scurry,
Isabel had a cleverer scheme;
She just woke up and fooled that dream.

Silverly

DENNIS LEE

Silverly,
　　Silverly,
Over the
　　Trees
The moon drifts
　　By on a
Runaway
　　Breeze.

Dozily,
　　Dozily,
Deep in her
　　Bed,
A little girl
　　Dreams with the
Moon in her
　　Head.

The Rabbit in the Moon

TRADITIONAL JAPANESE STORY retold by Florence Sakade

ONCE the Old-Man-of-the-Moon looked down into a big forest on the earth. He saw a rabbit and a monkey and a fox all living there together in the forest as very good friends.

"Now, I wonder which of them is the kindest," he said to himself. "I think I'll go down and see."

So the old man changed himself into a beggar and came down from the moon to the forest where the three animals were.

"Please help me," he said to them. "I'm very, very hungry."

"Oh! what a poor old beggar!" they said, and then they went hurrying off to find some food for the beggar.

The monkey brought a lot of fruit. And the fox caught a big fish. But the rabbit couldn't find anything at all to bring.

"Oh my! Oh my! What shall I do?" the rabbit cried. But just then he got an idea.

"Please, Mr Monkey," the rabbit said, "you gather some firewood for me. And you, Mr Fox, please make a big fire with the wood."

They did as the rabbit asked, and when the fire was burning very brightly, the rabbit said to the beggar, "I don't have anything to give you. So I'll put myself in this fire, and then when I'm cooked you can eat me."

The rabbit was about to jump into the fire and cook himself. But just then the beggar suddenly changed himself back into the Old-Man-of-the-Moon.

"You're very kind, Mr Rabbit," the Old Man said. "But you should never do anything to harm yourself. Since you're the kindest of all, I'll take you home to live with me."

Then the Old-Man-of-the-Moon took the rabbit in his arms and carried him up to the moon. Just look and see! If you look carefully at the moon when it is shining brightly, you can still see the rabbit there where the old man put him so very long ago.

Cat in the Dark

JOHN AGARD

Look at that!
Look at that!

But when you look
there's no cat.

Without a purr
just a flash of fur
and gone
like a ghost.

The most
you see
are two tiny
green traffic lights
staring at the night.

The Little Witch

MARGARET MAHY

THE big city was dark. Even the streetlights were out. All day people had gone up and down, up and down; cars and trams and trams and buses had roared and rattled busily along. But now they had all gone home to bed, and only the wind, the shadows, and a small kitten wandered in the wide, still streets.

The kitten chased a piece of paper, pretending it was a mouse. He patted at it with his paws and it flipped behind a rubbish bin. Quick as a wink he leaped after it, and then forgot it because he had found something else.

"What is this," he asked the wind, "here asleep behind the rubbish bin? I have never seen it before."

The wind was bowling a newspaper along, but he dropped it and came to see. The great stalking shadows looked down from everywhere.

"Ah," said the wind, "it is a witch . . . see her broomstick . . . but she is only a very small one."

The wind was right. It was a very small witch — a baby one.

The little witch heard the wind in her sleep and opened her eyes. Suddenly she was awake.

Far above, the birds peered down at the street below.

"Look!" said the shadows to the sparrows under the eaves. "Look at the little witch; she is such a little witch to be all alone."

"Let me see!" a baby sparrow peeped sleepily.

"Go to sleep!" said his mother. "I didn't hatch you out of the egg to peer at witches all night long."

She snuggled him back into her warm feathers.

But there was no one to snuggle a little witch, wandering cold in the big empty street, dragging a broom several sizes too big for her. The kitten sprang at the broom. Then he noticed something.

"Wind!" he cried. "See! Wherever this witch walks, she leaves a trail of flowers!"

Yes, it was true! The little witch had lots of magic in her, but she had not learned to use it properly, or to hide it, any more than she had learned to talk.

So wherever she put her feet mignonette grew, and rosemary, violets, lily-of-the-valley, and tiny pink-and-white roses . . . all through the streets, all across the road . . . .

Butterflies came, from far and wide, to dance and drink.

"Who is that down there?" asked a young moth.

"It is a baby witch who has made these fine, crimson feast-rooms for us," a tattered old moth answered.

The wind followed along, playing and juggling with the flowers and their sweet smells. "I shall sweep these all over the city," he said. In their sleep, people smelled the flowers and smiled, dreaming happily.

Now the witch looked up at the tall buildings; windows looked down at her with scorn, and their square sharp shapes seemed angry to her. She pointed her finger at them.

Out of the cracks and chinks suddenly crept long twining vines and green leaves. Slowly flowers opened on them . . . great crimson flowers like roses, smelling of honey.

The little witch laughed, but in a moment she became solemn. She was so alone. Then the kitten scuttled and pounced at her bare, pink heels, and the little witch knew she had a friend. Dragging her broom for the kitten to chase, she wandered on, leaving a trail of flowers.

Now the little witch stood in the street, very small and lost, and cold in her blue smock and bare feet.

She pointed up at the city clock-tower, and it became a huge fir tree, while the clock-face turned into a white nodding owl and flew away!

The owl flew as fast as the wind to a tall dark castle perched high on a hill. There at the window sat a slim, tired witch-woman, looking out into the night. "Where, oh where is my little baby witch? I must go and search for her again."

"Whoo! Whoo!" cried the owl. "There is a little witch down in the city and she is enchanting everything. What will the people say tomorrow?"

The witch-woman rode her broomstick through the sky and over the city, looking eagerly down through the mists. Far below she could see the little witch running and hiding in doorways, while the kitten chased after her.

Down flew the witch-woman — down, down to a shop doorway. The little witch and the kitten stopped and stared at her.

"Why," said the witch-woman, in her dark velvety voice, "you are my own dear little witch ... my little lost witch!"

She held out her arms and the little witch ran into them. She wasn't lost any more.

The witch-woman looked around at the enchanted city, and she smiled. "I'll leave it as it is," she said, "for a surprise tomorrow."

Then she gathered the little witch on to her broomstick, and the kitten jumped on, too, and off they went to their tall castle home, with windows as deep as night, and lived there happily ever after.

And the next day when the people got up and came out to work, the city was full of flowers and the echoes of laughter.

Come, Let's to Bed

TRADITIONAL RHYME

"Come, let's to bed,"
Says Sleepy-head;
"Tarry a while," says Slow;
"Hang on the pot,"
Says Greedy-gut,
"We'll sup before we go."

"To bed, to bed,"
Cried Sleepy-head,
But all the rest said, "No!
It is morning now;
You must milk the cow,
And tomorrow to bed we go."

tarry: wait

40

The Snooks Family

HARCOURT WILLIAMS

ONE night Mr and Mrs Snooks were going to bed as usual. It so happened that Mrs Snooks got into bed first, and she said to her husband, "Please, Mr Snooks, would you blow the candle out?" And Mr Snooks replied, "Certainly, Mrs Snooks." Whereupon he picked up the candlestick and began to blow, but unfortunately he could only blow by putting his under lip over his upper lip, which meant that his breath went up to the ceiling instead of blowing out the candle flame.

And he puffed and he puffed and he puffed, but he could not blow it out.

So Mrs Snooks said, "I will do it, my dear," and she got out of bed and took the candlestick from her husband and began to blow. But unfortunately she could only blow by putting her upper lip over her under lip, so that all her breath went down on to the floor. And she puffed and she puffed, but she could not blow the candle out.

So Mrs Snooks called their son John. John put on his sky-blue dressing-gown and slipped his feet into his primrose-coloured slippers and came down into his parents' bedroom.

"John, dear," said Mrs Snooks, "will you please blow out the candle for us?" And John said, "Certainly, Mummy."

But unfortunately John could only blow out of the right corner of his mouth, so that all his breath hit the wall of the room instead of the candle.

And he puffed and he puffed and he puffed, but he could not blow out the candle.

So they all called for his sister, little Ann. And little Ann put on her scarlet dressing-gown and slipped on her pink slippers and came down to her parents' bedroom.

"Ann, dear," said Mr Snooks, "will you please blow the candle out for us?" And Ann said, "Certainly, Daddy."

But unfortunately Ann could only blow out of the left side of her mouth, so that all her breath hit the wall instead of the candle.

And she puffed and she puffed and she puffed, but she could not blow out the candle.

It was just then that they heard in the street below a heavy steady tread coming along the pavement. Mr Snooks threw open the window and they all craned their heads out. They saw a policeman coming slowly towards the house.

"Oh, Mr Policeman," said Mrs Snooks, "will you come up and blow out our candle? We do so want to go to bed."

"Certainly, Madam," replied the policeman, and he entered and climbed the stairs – blump, blump, blump. He came into the bedroom where Mr Snooks, Mrs Snooks, John Snooks and little Ann Snooks were all standing round the candle which they could *not* blow out.

The policeman then picked up the candlestick in a very dignified manner and, putting his mouth into the usual shape for blowing, puffed out the candle at the first puff. Just like this – PUFF!

Then the Snooks family all said, "Thank you, Mr Policeman." And the policeman said, "Don't mention it," and turned to go down the stairs again.

"Just a moment, Mr Policeman," said Mr Snooks. "You mustn't go down the stairs in the dark. You might fall." And taking a box of matches, he LIT THE CANDLE AGAIN!

Mr Snooks went down the stairs with the policeman and saw him out of the door. His footsteps went blump, blump, blump along the quiet street.

John Snooks and little Ann Snooks went back to bed. Mr and Mrs Snooks got into bed again. There was silence for a moment.

"Mr Snooks," said Mrs Snooks, "would you blow out the candle?"

Mr Snooks got out of bed. "Certainly, Mrs Snooks," he said. . . .

And so the story started all over again.

44

Star Light

TRADITIONAL RHYME

Star light, star bright,
First star I see tonight,
I wish I may, I wish I might,
Have the wish I wish tonight.

Anansi and Candlefly

TRADITIONAL CARIBBEAN STORY retold by Philip Sherlock

IN the land where Anansi the Spiderman lived the nights were dark dark dark. There in the forest everything was wrapped in pitchy blackness and the animals couldn't see a paw's length in front of their noses. There were no lamps and no torches, just a few tiny creatures who carried their own light with them. One of these was Candlefly.

Candlefly always had fire, and the beam of her light shone in front of her as she moved through the night. If Dog had to be out late he got Candlefly to go ahead and light the way through the bush. Whenever Mrs Pig knew that she would be late getting back from the market, she paid Candlefly to light her safely past the deep hole by the mango tree and through the fields of damp guinea-grass by the edge of the precipice. Candlefly was always happy to help anyone, anyone except Anansi the Spiderman that is. And this is how it happened.

One day when Anansi ran out of matches, he ran across to Candlefly's house for help.

"Give me a piece of old firestick, Candlefly," said Anansi. "Any old piece will do.

46

It's time for us to start cooking our dinner, but we have no fire."

Candlefly gave Anansi the fire and, being generous, offered him some eggs.

Well, Anansi was greedy greedy and he loved eggs.

"Would I like some eggs, Candlefly? I'd love some eggs," he said. "Why only the other day Dr Humming-Bird was telling me that I should eat as many eggs as I could get."

So Candlefly gave Anansi some eggs and off he went with the eggs and the fire.

Next day Anansi was back.

"Oh, Candlefly," he said, "I need more fire and, by the way, those eggs you gave me yesterday were very good, very good indeed. Tell me, Candlefly, where do you get your eggs?"

Well, Candlefly gave Anansi some more fire and four more eggs but she didn't tell him how she got the eggs.

Anansi was back again the following day. Again he asked for fire and again Candlefly gave it to him, but this time she only gave him one egg. Well, Anansi didn't think much of that. Half-way home he stopped, put out the fire, and ate the egg. Then he went back to Candlefly.

"Look," he complained, "the fire was no good. It went out."

Candlefly gave him more fire and Anansi waited for her to give him another egg. He waited and he waited, but Candlefly took no notice of him and just went on with her work. Finally he said, "Oh, Ouch, Cousin Candlefly! The fire has burnt my hand! Quick, give me an egg so I can put some egg-yolk on the burn to heal it."

"All right, Anansi," replied Candlefly. "I will give you another egg and, since you like eggs so much, how would you like me to show you a place where you can get as many eggs as you like, as easy as can be?"

Well, this was what Anansi had been waiting for.

"When can we start?" he said.

"Well," said Candlefly, "I can't take you to the place by day, only after nightfall, so come back tomorrow when it's dark and not before."

Anansi couldn't wait. All the next day he walked about restlessly, longing for evening. Before it was even lunchtime he had been to the village to borrow the largest bag he could find from Shopkeeper Dog. After lunch he kept going outside looking up at the sun and wishing it would move more quickly across the sky. It was still only three o'clock and the sun was still high when he walked across to Candlefly's house and sat down under an ackee tree to wait.

"That's a big bag, Anansi!" called Candlefly. "But you'll have to wait. We can't go before nightfall."

Anansi sat under the shade of the tree, picking away at the

blades of guinea-grass and praying for night to come. He saw the sun sink behind the mountain and heard Cricket beginning to tune up in the bush by the side of the road. "Hurry up!" he shouted. "Hurry up!" He heard tree-frog begin to whistle from the branch of the ackee tree, saw the first star come out in the deep-blue sky above and felt the night breeze stir the leaves. "You're lazy and slow," complained Anansi. "Hurry up!" He was so busy shouting at them all that he nearly didn't hear Candlefly when she called:

"Ready now, Anansi? It's time to go."

The two set off down the road in the dark, Candlefly in front with her beam of light, Anansi behind her with his long bag. They walked and they walked and after an hour they came to Egg Valley.

"Here we are," said Candlefly and shone her beam around until it lit on an egg.

Quick as a flash Anansi called out, "It's mine, it's mine! I saw it first!" and, pushing Candlefly out of the way, he grabbed the egg and put it in his bag.

The same thing happened with the next egg and the next. Each time Anansi shouted, "It's mine, it's mine! I saw it first!" Soon he had fifty eggs while Candlefly had none, but Candlefly being weaker than Anansi couldn't take the eggs away from him.

When Anansi had about a hundred eggs in the bag, Candlefly, who had none, turned to him and said, "Well, Mr Anansi, since you're so greedy you will just have to find your own way home without a light. Good night." And off she flew.

It was a dark dark night and Anansi couldn't see a thing. He wasn't sure which way to go or where to put his foot. Above all he didn't want to spoil the eggs in his bag.

"Poor me," muttered Anansi. "What a wicked creature that Candlefly is, leaving me all in darkness. Poor me."

Very very slowly, straining his eyes to try and see in the dark, Anansi set off. He tripped and stumbled every step of the way and before he'd gone very far he walked smack! into the side of a small house.

From inside came a growling roaring voice that Anansi knew and feared.

"Who is that coming here at this time of night?" it growled. "Who's that?"

"It's me, Godfather Tiger," said Anansi, thinking fast. "And . . . and I've brought some lovely eggs for you!"

"Grrmph," replied Tiger. "I'll get a light. But if you're fooling, there will be TROUBLE!"

A few moments later the door opened.

Out came Tiger, angry at being woken up.

"Good morning, Tiger," said Anansi, shaking with fear. "Here are the eggs I brought for you."

"Good morning nothing!" shouted Tiger. "It's not morning. It's the middle of the night. Come in and let me see the eggs. I don't trust you at all."

Tiger held open the door for Anansi to go in, shut it firmly behind him and stood over him as Anansi took the eggs out of his bag one by one.

"Look at them, Godfather Tiger," he said. "Look what lovely eggs they are. I know how you like eggs. When I saw these I said to myself, 'Godfather Tiger and Godmother Tiger will enjoy these.'"

Well, Tiger and his wife set to and cooked the eggs and when they were ready Tiger said, "Do you want some, Anansi?"

Did Anansi want some eggs!? Oh how he wanted some eggs! But he was much too frightened to say anything except, "Oh no, Godfather Tiger, I brought the eggs for you. I don't want any."

So Tiger and his wife ate all the eggs and very good they were too.

But Tiger was still cross about being woken up and, knowing how greedy greedy Anansi was, he didn't believe his story for a minute. So he thought of a plan to catch him out.

Sending Anansi out of the room for some water, he carefully took two of the empty egg shells and put them back into the pot, arranging them so that they looked as if they had never been eaten. At the bottom of the pot he hid a small live lobster with pinchy squinchy claws. Then he called Anansi and, making sure he saw the two eggs at the bottom of the pot, he said, "Come and lie down here beside me, Anansi, I'm going to put out the light."

No sooner had Tiger put out the light than Anansi, who was feeling very very hungry, reached out, felt for the rim of the pot and put his hand down to take out an egg. The lobster pinched him sharply. Anansi almost jumped out of the bed with pain and fright.

"What's the matter with you, Mr Anansi?" growled Tiger.

"Oh, nothing nothing, Godfather Tiger. It must have been a flea from your dog that bit me as I was falling asleep," said Anansi.

"Well, don't wake me up again," said Tiger.

A few minutes later Anansi tried to take an egg out of the pot again, and again the lobster nipped him, this time even more sharply.

"Ouch!" cried Anansi. "Oh, what a lot of fleas there are in this bed. What a lot of fleas!"

Anansi and Tiger had a restless night. In the morning Tiger said, "You're the first person who's ever complained about fleas biting him in my house."

"Oh, Godfather Tiger," replied Anansi, "I got very little sleep last night and I'm very tired. Now the daylight's here I think I'll go home."

"Is that so?" growled Tiger. "Well, I'm not so sure I'm going to let you go. What were you trying to steal out of the pot last night?"

Well, when Anansi realized he'd been found out he was almost scared out of his wits. He ran out of the door and home as fast as he could, with his empty belly aching at the thought of all those lovely eggs; and Tiger just laughed and licked his lips.

After that Anansi often tried to persuade Candlefly to take him back to Egg Valley. He promised he would only take his fair share. But Candlefly wouldn't take him and, to this day, Anansi is the only person to whom she will not give a light.

Escape at Bedtime

ROBERT LOUIS STEVENSON

The lights from the parlour and kitchen shone out
    Through the blinds and the windows and bars;
And high overhead and all moving about,
    There were thousands of millions of stars.
There ne'er were such thousands of leaves on a tree,
    Nor of people in church or the Park,
As the crowds of the stars that looked down upon me,
    And that glittered and winked in the dark.

The Dog, and the Plough, and the Hunter, and all,
    And the star of the sailor, and Mars,
These shone in the sky, and the pail by the wall
    Would be half full of water and stars.
They saw me at last, and they chased me with cries,
    And they soon had me packed into bed;
But the glory kept shining and bright in my eyes,
    And the stars going round in my head.

Half a Kingdom

TRADITIONAL ICELANDIC STORY retold by Ann McGovern

WHEN you wake up in the morning you never can tell what might happen to you during the day.

One fine morning, Prince Lini woke up in his castle on the hill. He didn't have the slightest idea what was going to happen to him that day. He was riding in the forest with his friends, when, suddenly, a thick, cold fog blew into the woods and covered the prince from head to toe.

A minute later, it drifted away and was gone. Gone, too, was Prince Lini. His friends searched for him all day and all night. And, in the morning, they rode to the castle to tell the king about the fog that rolled in from the sky and took away his son.

Now the king loved his son more than anything, even more than the riches of his kingdom. He sent for his strongest and wisest men.

"Whoever finds Prince Lini," he said, "and brings him back to me, will win half my kingdom."

All over the kingdom, people heard the news that the prince had disappeared.

Now because the king loved his riches so much, almost everyone in the kingdom was poor. So almost everyone took part in the search.

One fine morning, a poor peasant girl called Signy woke up in her cottage at the edge of the forest. She didn't have the slightest idea what was going to happen to her that day. Then she heard about the missing prince and the king's reward of half a kingdom.

She knew that the strongest and wisest men had looked far and wide.

"I'll look near and narrow," she thought.

Signy knew the secret places of the forest better than anyone else. So she set off to search for Prince Lini.

All that day she searched. She saw nothing but tree shapes in the snow. She heard nothing but the song of the icy wind.

As it grew dark, Signy made for her favourite, warm cave and peered inside. There, stretched out on a golden bed, fast asleep, was Prince Lini. She tried to wake him. But he slept on, in a deep, deep sleep.

All of a sudden she heard a clattering and a chattering. She ran to hide in the darkest corner of the cave. Two trolls entered; one tall, one small. They whistled.

Signy listened carefully to the tune. Two swans flew into the cave and the trolls chanted:

Sing, O sing, O swans of mine,
Sing Prince Lini awake.

The swans sang.

Prince Lini stirred, rubbed his eyes and sat up.

"Now," said the trolls, "for the ninety-seventh time, will you marry one of us?"

"Never," replied the prince.

"You'll be sorry," said the tall troll.

Then she commanded the swans:

Sing, O sing, O swans of mine,
Sing Prince Lini asleep.

Prince Lini slept and the swans flew away.

The next morning, when the trolls left the cave, Signy whistled the same tune. The swans flew into the cave and she said:

Sing, O sing, O swans of mine,
Sing Prince Lini awake.

The swans sang.

Prince Lini stirred, rubbed his eyes, sat up and rubbed his eyes again.

"Who are you?" he asked.

"Signy," she said. "And I've come to take you home. Your father's so miserable without you. He's even offered half his kingdom to whoever finds you."

"I don't know that I want to be found," said the prince. "You see, I hate the way the kingdom is run. The rich are too rich and hardly work at all. The poor are too poor and work all the time."

"Yes," said Signy sadly. "Everyone I know is poor."

"But, wait a minute, you won't be poor if you get half the kingdom – and you can share it with everyone! Oh, Signy, take me back and claim half the kingdom. Please."

"The first thing is to get you out of here," she said.

"Let's go then," said the prince.

"No," said Signy, "the trolls will send their magic fog to capture us. But I've an idea . . . ." She told him her plan and he agreed. Then Signy whistled, and the swans sang Prince Lini to sleep. And again she hid in the dark corner.

Soon the trolls entered and woke Prince Lini in the usual way.
And they asked him their usual question.

"Now, for the ninety-eighth time, will you marry one of us?"

"Tell me," he said, "where do you go and what do you do during the day?"

"We go to the big oak tree in the middle of the forest and throw our giant, golden egg to and fro, to and fro," said the small troll.

"What happens if you drop it?" Prince Lini asked.

"Oh, we never drop it. If it breaks, we would disappear."

"Enough chatter," interrupted the tall troll.

"Now, for the ninety-ninth time, will you marry one of us?"

"Never, never, never, never, never!" replied the prince.

"You'll be very sorry," they snarled. Then they whistled and the swans sang Prince Lini to sleep.

The next morning, Signy and Prince Lini followed the trolls to the middle of the forest. They watched them throw a giant, golden egg to and fro, to and fro.

Signy signalled to Prince Lini. He picked up a stone. He aimed carefully and threw it. The stone shattered the giant, golden egg and it fell to the ground in a shower of little pieces.

Suddenly, from nowhere, a thick cold fog blew into the woods and covered the trolls from head to toe. A minute later, it drifted away and was gone. Gone, too, were the trolls. Signy and Prince Lini ran all the way to the palace.

"Wait outside," Signy told the prince. And she went to see his father alone.

"What do you want?" asked the king.

"I want half your kingdom, for I've found your son," Signy replied.

61

"Don't be silly," said the king. "How can a girl find my son when my strongest and wisest men could not? It cannot be true."

Signy ran to the door and flung it open. There stood the prince. The king hugged his son and cried tears of happiness.

"Now will you give up half your kingdom?" Signy asked.

"My precious kingdom," the king sighed.

"What about your precious son and your promise?" said the prince.

The king looked at Signy carefully.

"A peasant girl found my son – not even a princess! But my precious son is right. And a promise is a promise. I'll give you half my kingdom."

Prince Lini turned to Signy. "I'll help to run your half a kingdom, if you like," he offered.

Signy thought for a moment and said:

"We can share half the kingdom and make it a fairer place, where people are neither rich nor poor. And we can share adventures too!"

And that's exactly what they did, happily and for ever.

So, when you wake in the morning – tomorrow morning – you never can tell what might happen to you during the day.

Hush You My Babby

TRADITIONAL

Hush you my babby
Lie still with your daddy
Your mother has gone to the mill
To get you some wheat
To make you some meat
So hush you my babby, lie still.

Bye Baby Bunting

TRADITIONAL

Bye baby bunting
Daddy's gone a-hunting
Mother's gone a-milking
Sister's gone a-silking
Brother's gone to get a skin
To wrap the baby bunting in
So bye baby bunting.

meat: food   bye: sleep

63

Hush Little Baby

TRADITIONAL AMERICAN

Hush little baby, don't say a word
Poppa's gonna buy you a mocking bird
And if that mocking bird won't sing
Poppa's gonna buy you a diamond ring
And if that diamond ring turns to brass
Poppa's gonna buy you a looking glass
And if that looking glass gets broke
Poppa's gonna buy you a billy goat
And if that billy goat runs away
Poppa's gonna buy you another today
So hush little baby don't say a word
Cos Poppa's gonna buy you a mocking bird.

Hush-a-ba Birdie

TRADITIONAL SCOTS

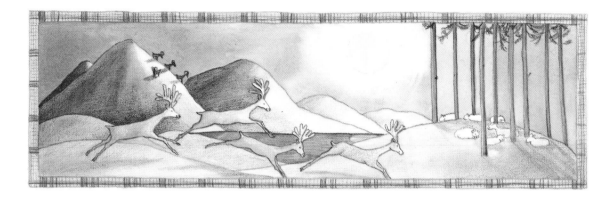

Hush-a-ba birdie croon, croon,
Hush-a-ba birdie croon.
The sheep have gone to the silver wood
And the kye have gone to the broom, broom,
The kye have gone to the broom.

Oh and it's braw milking kye, kye,
Oh and it's braw milking kye.
The birds are singing, the bells are ringing
And the wild deer come galloping by, by,
The wild deer come galloping by.

Hush-a-ba birdie croon, croon,
Hush-a-ba birdie croon.
The goats have gone to the mountains high
And they won't be hame until noon, noon,
They won't be hame until noon.

kye: cows   braw: fine   hame: home

Goodnight

THOMAS HOOD

Here's a body – there's a bed,
There's a pillow – here's a head,
There's a curtain – here's a light,
There's a puff – and so goodnight!

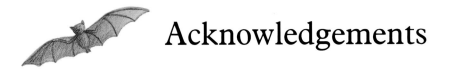# Acknowledgements

The Publishers gratefully acknowledge permission to reproduce the following:

"Dream Variations," copyright © 1926 by Alfred A. Knopf, Inc, and renewed 1954 by Langston Hughes. Reprinted from *Selected Poems of Langston Hughes*, by permission of Alfred A. Knopf, Inc.

"The Crow and the Daylight" was first published in *To Read And To Tell*, ed. Norah Montgomerie (The Bodley Head, 1962). Reprinted by permission of Norah Montgomerie.

"I'm the Big Sleeper" by Michael Rosen was first published in *Mind Your Own Business* (1974). Reprinted by permission of André Deutsch Ltd.

"I Like To Stay Up," copyright © Grace Nichols 1984 is reprinted by permission of Curtis Brown Group Ltd. on behalf of Grace Nichols.

"The Fly-By-Night" was first published in *Fairy Tales*, by Terry Jones (1981). Reprinted by permission of Pavilion Books and Alfred A. Knopf, Inc.

"Bump" by Spike Milligan from *Silly Verse for Kids*, is reprinted by permission of Spike Milligan Productions Limited.

The extract from "The Adventures of Isabel" is reprinted by permission of Curtis Brown Group Ltd., copyright © 1936 by Ogden Nash.